SUPER SPORTS STAR

ICHIRO SUZUKI

Ken Rappoport

Enslow Publishers, Inc.

40 Industrial Road   PO Box 38
Box 398   Aldershot
Berkeley Heights, NJ 07922   Hants GU12 6BP
USA   UK

http://www.enslow.com

Library of Congress Cataloging-in-Publication Data

Rappoport, Ken.
   Super sports star Ichiro Suzuki / Ken Rappoport.
     p. cm. — (Super sports star)
   Summary: A biography of the Seattle Mariners hitting and fielding star who won the MVP and Rookie of the Year Award in 2001 after a hugely successful career playing baseball in his native Japan.
   Includes bibliographical references (p.) and index.
   ISBN 0-7660-2137-8
   1. Suzuki, Ichiro, 1973—-Juvenile literature. 2. Baseball players—Japan—Biography—Juvenile literature. [1. Suzuki, Ichiro, 1973- 2. Baseball players. 3. Japan—Biography.] I. Title: Ichiro Suzuki. II. Title. III. Series.
GV865.S895R36   2004
796.357'092—dc21

2003010326

Printed in the United States of America

10 9 8 7 6 5 4 3 2 1

To Our Readers:
We have done our best to make sure all Internet Addresses in this book were active and appropriate when we went to press. However, the author and the publisher have no control over and assume no liability for the material available on those Internet sites or on other Web sites they may link to. Any comments or suggestions can be sent by e-mail to comments@enslow.com or to the address on the back cover.

Photo Credits: © 2002 Grieshop/MLB Photos, p. 40; © Andy Hayt/MLB Photos, p. 35; © 2002 Andy Hayt/MLB Photos, p. 12; © Rob Leiter/MLB Photos, p. 1; © 2002 Brad Mangin/MLB Photos, p. 18; © 2002 MLB Photos, p. 32; © 2001 Rich Pilling/MLB Photos, p. 14; © 2002 Rich Pilling/MLB Photos, pp. 4, 10, 29; © Don Smith/MLB Photos, p. 22; © 2002 Ben VanHouten/MLB Photos, pp. 26, 30, 38; © 2002 Ron Vesely/MLB Photos, pp. 20, 45; © 2002 Williamson/MLB Photos, p. 24; © 2002 Michael Zagaris/MLB Photos, pp. 8, 39.

Cover Photo: © Rob Leiter/MLB Photos.

CONTENTS

Introduction

At 5-foot-9 and 160 pounds, Ichiro Suzuki looks like the batboy. But he is not. He is one of the most feared players in baseball.

He starred for many years in Japan. In only one season he became a star in the major leagues. And he did it his way.

He is the right fielder for the Seattle Mariners. He is the first non-pitcher from Japan to play in the big leagues. He is the first player to wear his first name on his uniform. He shows American fans you do not have to hit home runs all the time to create excitement.

Ichiro uses his bat like a magic wand. Ichiro (as he likes to be called) lays down perfectly placed bunts. He beats out perfectly placed grounders for hits. He sprays line drives all over the field. He can also hit a home run when needed.

He steals games with his daring base

running. He saves games with his powerful throws from the outfield. He has quickly become one of the best players in the game.

When he played in Japan, Ichiro was like a rock star. He had millions of fans. In America, he has won new fans with his daring play.

Ichiro-mania

"I-CHI-RO! I-CHI-RO!"

Fans cheered. They waved Japanese flags. Flashbulbs popped. It was the 2001 All-Star Game in Seattle. Ichiro Suzuki walked to the plate. This was the moment everyone was waiting for.

Ichiro was playing in his first All-Star Game in the major leagues. But he was no stranger to All-Star games. In Japan, he won seven straight batting titles and three Most Valuable Player awards. He played in seven All-Star games there.

Now he was in the majors with the Seattle Mariners. He wanted to test himself against the best.

The Mariners hoped Ichiro would be a good player for them. He did more than expected. At the All-Star break, he was leading the American League in batting, hits, and steals. Ichiro pulled

Ichiro rounds the bases hoping to score.

in more All-Star votes from the fans than any other player. "This guy is one of the top five players in the world," said New York Mets catcher Mike Piazza.

Ichiro's fast start quickly won over the fans in Seattle. Behind his position in right field at SAFECO Field, the section is called "Area 51." That is Ichiro's uniform number. Fans hang signs such as "Ichiro MVP." They cheer for their hero.

Now he was playing on his home field in the All-Star Game. Ichiro dug into the batter's box to face Randy Johnson. Johnson once pitched for Seattle. Now he pitched for Arizona. It was an old Mariners star against the new Mariners star.

Johnson wound up and fired. Ball one. The next pitch came in. Ichiro hit a sharp grounder to deep first. Todd Helton

★★★ **UP CLOSE**

When he lived in Japan, Ichiro watched a lot of major league All-Star Games. He said it gave him a good feeling about baseball in America.

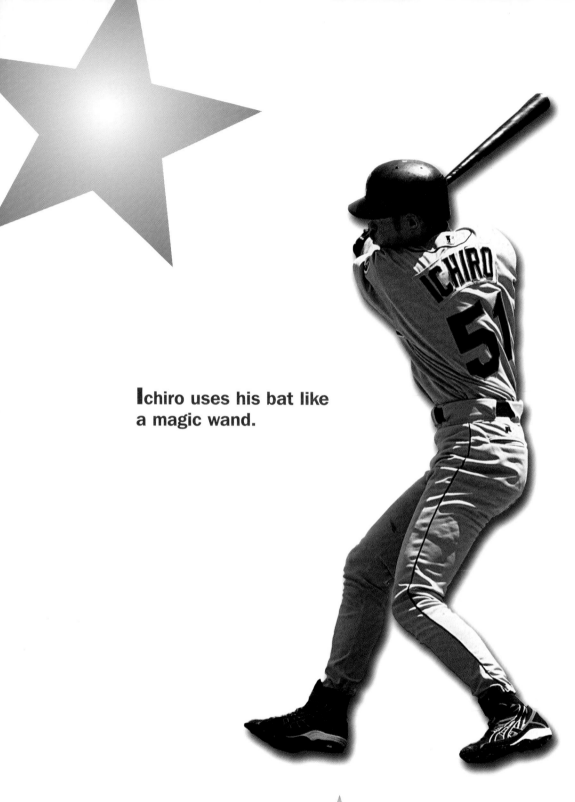

Ichiro uses his bat like
a magic wand.

fielded the ball. But Ichiro was across the bag before Helton could toss to Johnson. A single in his very first All-Star at bat. "He got the base hit because he's so fast," Johnson said. Ichiro then showed more of his speed. He stole second base.

A hit. A steal. It was Ichiro, as expected. And the sellout crowd of 47,364 went home happy after the AL's 4–1 win. Ichiro showed he could play with the best in the majors, just as he had shown for many years in Japan.

Small Steps

In Japan, it was "Ichiro-mania." He could not go anywhere without being mobbed by fans. Ichiro played for the Orix Blue Wave. He was the only player in Japan's Pacific League to wear just his first name on his uniform. The top ticket for home games at Kobe Green Stadium was in the right field bleachers. The fans wanted to be close to him.

His name is pronounced "EE-chi-ro." It means "First Boy" in Japanese. The family name of Suzuki means "sacred tree." It is one of the most popular names in Japan. Ichiro's family has been traced to a 12th century samurai warrior. It is fitting. At the plate he handles the bat like a warrior's weapon. He is one of the best bunters in baseball. He can hit the ball to all fields. And he hardly ever strikes out.

Ichiro has worked very hard to become a great baseball player.

How did he get to be the top baseball player in Japan? Ichiro has worked very hard at baseball since he was a young boy.

He was born on October 22, 1973. He lived in Toyoyama. The town is located near the city of Nagoya in central Japan.

When he was three years old he was given a red leather glove and baseball by his father, Nobuyuki. Ichiro was happy. To him the glove and ball were treasures. They rarely left his side. When Ichiro was eight he joined the town baseball team. His father became the team manager.

Ichiro's father worked in a factory. But he always found time to take his son to the baseball field to practice. Father and son worked on every part of the game—hitting, fielding, pitching, and running. Ichiro was a natural runner with great speed. He loved to run. His boyhood hero was Olympic track and field star Carl Lewis.

Ichiro would go to batting cages to get his timing down. The pitches from the machine came in faster and faster. The pitches went from 60 to 70 to 80 miles per hour. Before long he was able to hit the fastest pitches.

"From my earliest days playing, it's always been baseball," he said. "At each level I played, I fell in love with the game all over again."

Following a Dream

Ichiro had his heart set on a baseball career. He attended Aikodai Meiden High School. It was known for a strong baseball program. It was scary for Ichiro. He had to move away from home. But there was no time to be homesick. He was busy with baseball and schoolwork.

Coach Go Nakamura had already sent eleven players to the pros. He knew talent when he saw it. But when he first looked at Ichiro, he was shocked. Could this small, thin kid make it? Yes, he could. Ichiro's fastball was timed at 93 miles per hour. That was as fast as a pitcher in the major leagues! And he could really swing the bat. Twice he played in Koshien. That is the National High School baseball tournament in Japan. As a senior he hit .700 in the tournament.

Ichiro played in Japan's National High School baseball tournament two times.

Then Ichiro's dream came true. In 1992, he was drafted by the Orix Blue Wave. The Blue Wave play in Japan's Pacific League.

At first Ichiro had a small problem. The Blue Wave batting coach tried to change his batting style. Ichiro was a left-handed hitter with an unusual batting stance. As he faced the pitcher he would lift his right leg high. He would swing it back and forth. It helped him to time the pitch. "It was part of my image," Ichiro said. "When you think of Ichiro, you think of the leg kick."

Ichiro also had different kinds of swings. "If something works, there's no need to change it," he said. He refused to change.

It took him three years to make the Blue

★ ★ ★ **UP CLOSE**

Ichiro has his own museum in Japan, opened by his father. Along with the usual collection of bats, balls, gloves, and trophies, the museum also features baby pictures, toys that Ichiro played with as a child, the bicycle he rode to elementary school, and school exams.

In 1992, Ichiro was drafted by the Orix Blue Wave in Japan's Pacific League.

Wave starting lineup. Now Ichiro was spraying line drives all over the field. He was beating out infield hits. He was hard to stop. His hit total piled up game after game. By the end of the 1994 season, he had 210 hits. It was a record for Nippon Professional Baseball. His .385 batting average led the Pacific League. That was also a record. He was named the PL's Most Valuable Player.

It was only the beginning.

Big Man In Japan

Heads turned in the Orix Blue Wave locker room. "My average is high enough," Ichiro said. "Now I'm going to start hitting home runs." Some of his teammates smiled. At 5-foot-9 and 160 pounds, Ichiro did not look like a power hitter like Barry Bonds or Mark McGwire. When Ichiro won the batting title and Most Valuable Player award in 1994 he had a record 210 hits. But only 13 of those were home runs. He was not thought of as a power hitter.

In 1995, Ichiro was heading toward another batting title. But suddenly he was surprising everyone with his power. By the end of the season he had cracked 25 home runs. That nearly doubled the total he had hit the year before.

It was just like Ichiro. He had simply said he was going to do something. And then he went ahead and did it!

Ichiro was more than just a good hitter. His blazing speed made him one of the league's top base stealers. His defense earned him a Gold Glove for the second straight year. The Gold Glove award is given to an outfielder who has played superbly. Base runners feared his strong throws from the outfield.

Ichiro swings at the ball.

Ichiro was in a class by himself. In 1995, he won another batting title. He won another MVP award. He did the same in 1996. The season was capped with a victory in the Japan Series. That is Japan's version of the World Series.

Now with a ring, Ichiro had it all. By 1996 he also had the record for baseball salaries in Japan. He was making $4.2 million a year. He had his own clothing line. His smiling face looked down from billboards. At 25, he had become the favorite of Japanese fans, especially with the younger fans. Ichiro liked to wear stylish sunglasses and his cap backwards. With his spiky hair, he looked like a rock star.

In 1999, he won his fifth straight batting title in Japan. The Seattle Mariners invited him to spring training in America. He impressed Mariners manager Lou Piniella.

"You could see that he was very confident," the manager said. Two years later, Ichiro was the starting right fielder for the Mariners.

CHAPTER 5

Coming to America

All eyes were on Ichiro Suzuki after he signed a contract in 2001 with the Seattle Mariners.

This was pressure. He had won seven batting titles and seven Gold Gloves in Japan. But now he had to prove himself all over again in the big leagues.

Other Japanese players had gone to America before him. They were all pitchers. Ichiro would be the first position player to make the jump.

Ichiro's favorite major-league player was Ken Griffey, Jr. He owned a Griffey uniform. When he put it on he had dreamed he was a big leaguer. And now he actually was.

Bringing Ichiro to Seattle was costly for the Mariners. First they paid the Orix Blue Wave. It was more than $13 million just to discuss a contract with him. Then they agreed to pay Ichiro over $15 million for three years.

Many big stars had worn Seattle uniforms in the past, from Griffey to Alex Rodriguez. Few had as much media attention as Ichiro. From the moment he walked onto the field in spring training, he was in the spotlight. Most of the reporters were from Japan. Dozens of cameramen followed him around. They recorded his every move. There was great interest in Japan about him. Too much, he thought. "I am used to a similar experience in Japan with the media around me all the time," he said. "But sometimes I get stressed out that I must talk every day."

Ichiro talked, but told little. He is a very private person. Reporters asked him

Ichiro started playing for the Seattle Mariners in 2001.

the name of his dog. He did not tell them. His personal life? All reporters could find out was that his favorite food was rice balls. And his wife, Yumiko, worked as a TV broadcaster.

Rather than talk to reporters, Ichiro preferred to sit at his locker. He would rub the bottoms of his feet with a piece of wood. He explained it helped to keep his feet soft. "If your feet are healthy, you are healthy," he said.

When the season started, Ichiro started getting more attention from the press. As the

Ichiro gets ready to throw the ball in from right field.

Mariners' leadoff hitter, he was on a streak. On May 15, the Mariners faced the Chicago White Sox. They fell behind 2–0 in the first inning. Then Ichiro came up in the bottom of the first. He singled to extend his hitting streak to 20 games. He later scored the Mariners' first run. In the ninth inning, Ichiro again was in the middle of the action. This time it was on defense. His perfect throw from right field helped to cut down a Chicago base runner. The throw helped the Mariners win, 4–3.

Ichiro was helping his team win in many ways. Could he keep it up?

A Season To Remember

Ichiro stepped to the plate. All eyes in the Seattle dugout were on the little leadoff batter. He swung and connected. Base hit! The players in the dugout slapped hands.

"We're all sitting in the dugout. We just start laughing when he gets the hit," said Mariners teammate Bret Boone. "He gets the ball rolling for us every time."

The Mariners were off to the best start in baseball in 2001. Ichiro was leading the way.

At the All-Star break, he had the most hits in the major leagues. He had scored the most runs. He was tied for first in steals. And he had one of the best batting averages at .347. To top it off, he got the most votes to play in the All-Star Game.

Ichiro had become the best leadoff hitter in baseball. He was one of the fastest runners going from home to first. He was so fast that he often beat out grounders or bunts for base hits.

Whenever Ichiro came up to bat, infielders moved a few steps closer to home. This gave them a better chance to throw him out on a ground ball. It usually worked for most hitters. But not always against Ichiro.

One day in Toronto, Ichiro was at bat. As always, the Blue Jay infielders moved in. Ichiro hit a grounder to Alex Gonzalez. The Toronto shortstop fielded the ball and fired to first. No luck. Ichiro beat the throw for a hit.

"That's his game," Gonzalez said. "He chops the ball and tries to beat it out."

But could he break Shoeless Joe Jackson's rookie record for hits in a season? It was one of baseball's oldest records. In 1911, Jackson had cracked 233 hits for the Cleveland Indians. The entire baseball world now watched as Ichiro closed in on the mark.

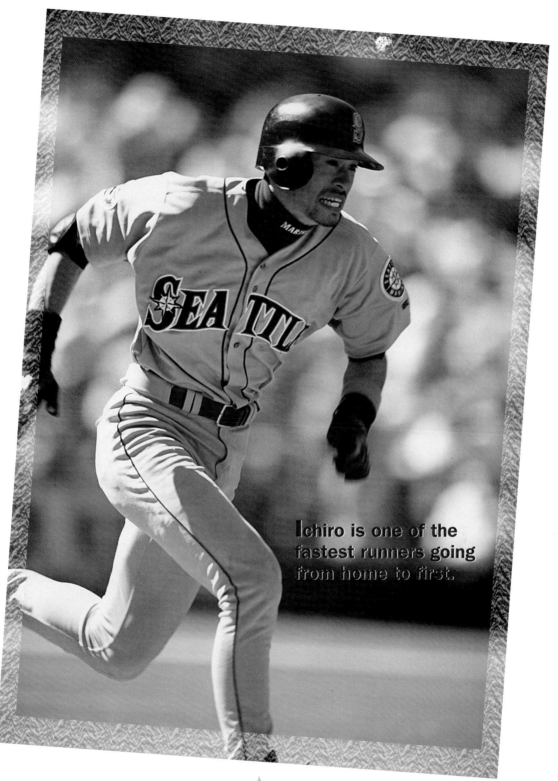

Ichiro is one of the fastest runners going from home to first.

It was late in September. Ichiro stepped in to bat against the Oakland Athletics. He slashed the ball to center. The ball dropped in for Ichiro's 234th hit. The record was his! The crowd at Seattle's SAFECO Field stood. "I-chir-o! I-chir-o! I-chir-o!" Ichiro took off his batting helmet. He waved to the fans.

"I didn't expect the standing ovation," he said through a translator. "I didn't know what to do at first after the fans started. I appreciate all the support the fans here have given me."

A week later the Mariners did something special as a team. They won their 116th game. It tied the major league record for most wins in a season. The record was set by the Chicago Cubs in 1906. Ichiro and the Mariners were now headed for the playoffs.

Rising To The Heights

Where was the Mariners' magic? Suddenly it was missing. One more loss to the Cleveland Indians and they would be out of the playoffs.

Game 4 of the series was tied 1–1 in the seventh. Ichiro stepped to the plate to face Cleveland ace Bartolo Colon. There were runners on first and second with two out. Ichiro swung. Base hit! It broke the tie. The Mariners scored another in the inning. They rallied for a 6–2 victory. Ichiro was red-hot. He finished the game with three hits.

Back to Seattle for the deciding game. Ichiro continued to hit the ball hard. In the first inning, he singled to short. In the third, he singled to second. In the seventh inning, he singled to short. He came around to score.

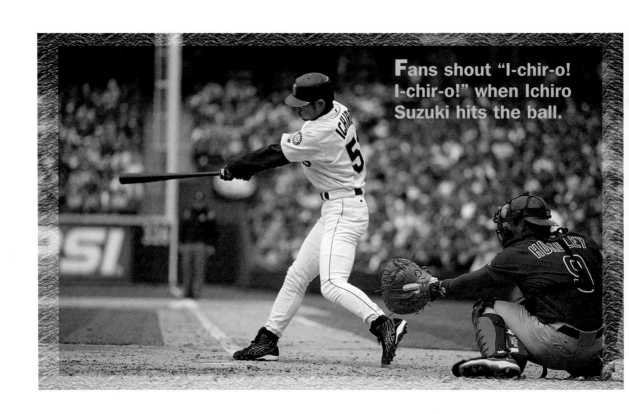

Fans shout "I-chir-o! I-chir-o!" when Ichiro Suzuki hits the ball.

They were on their way. The Mariners clinched the series with a 3–1 victory.

What a show by Ichiro! He batted .600. It was a record for a post-season series. His 12 hits also tied a post-season record held by teammate Edgar Martinez. This was his very first taste of playoff baseball in the majors. He was doing great, just as he had in Japan. "Ichiro is a rookie and he's playing like he's been playing in this league for 15 years," Martinez said.

The Mariners then lost to New York. But the 2001

Ichiro leaps for the ball in right field.

season had been an amazing year for the Mariners. It was amazing as well for their Japanese star. Ichiro led the American League with a .350 batting average and 242 hits. He won both the Most Valuable Player and Rookie of the Year awards. He was only the second player in major league history to do so.

He proved that his great rookie year was no accident. In 2002, Ichiro again walloped over 200 hits. He batted over .300. It is the measure for stardom in the big leagues.

As the 2003 season got underway, there was no drop-off in Ichiro's play. "Now that he's comfortable, he's just getting better every year," said one major-league scout.

When Ichiro first played in the major leagues, two nations were watching him. The pressure was building. He had been a huge star in Japan. Could he possibly be as good in the majors? That is what everyone asked. By the end of two seasons he had answered the question in a big way.

East or West, he was now one of the greatest players in the game.

CAREER STATISTICS

	Japan's Pacific Coast League											
Year	Team	G	AB	R	H	2B	3B	HR	RBI	BB	SB	Avg.
1992	Orix Blue Wave	40	95	9	24	5	0	0	5	3	3	.253
1993	Orix Blue Wave	43	64	4	12	2	0	1	3	2	0	.188
1994	Orix Blue Wave	130	546	111	210	41	5	13	54	51	29	.385
1995	Orix Blue Wave	130	524	104	179	23	4	25	80	68	49	.342
1996	Orix Blue Wave	130	542	104	193	24	4	16	84	56	35	.356
1997	Orix Blue Wave	135	536	94	185	31	4	17	91	62	39	.345
1998	Orix Blue Wave	135	506	79	181	36	3	13	71	43	11	.358
1999	Orix Blue Wave	103	411	80	141	27	2	21	68	45	12	.343
2000	Orix Blue Wave	105	395	73	153	22	1	12	73	54	21	.387
Totals		951	3,619	658	1,278	211	23	118	529	384	199	.353

CAREER STATISTICS

MLB–American League													
Year	Team	G	AB	R	H	2B	3B	HR	RBI	BB	SB	Avg.
2001	SEA	157	692	127	242	34	8	8	69	30	56	.350
2002	SEA	157	647	111	208	27	8	8	51	68	31	.321
Total		314	1,339	238	450	61	16	16	120	98	87	.336

G—Games   **HR**—Home Runs
AB—At Bats   **RBI**—Runs Batted In
R—Runs   **BB**—Bases on Balls (Walks)
H—Hits   **SB**—Stolen Bases
2B—Doubles   **Avg.**—Batting Average
3B—Triples

Where to Write to Ichiro Suzuki

Mr. Ichiro Suzuki
c/o The Seattle Mariners
SAFECO Field
1250 First Avenue S
Seattle, WA 98134

Ichiro is one of the greatest baseball players.

WORDS TO KNOW

All-Star Game—The mid-season game between the best players in the American and National Leagues. Fans vote for the players who start the game.

Gold Glove—The annual award given to the best fielder at his position.

Koshien—The National High School baseball tournament in Japan.

major leagues—The top professional league in baseball.

Most Valuable Player (MVP)—The annual award given to the best player in the league.

playoffs—After the regular season is over, four teams in each of the American and National Leagues compete for the world championship.

Rookie of the Year—The award given to the best first-year player in the league.

samurai warrior—Ancient Japanese warriors who fought their enemies with razor-sharp swords.

World Series—Each fall the champions of the American and National Leagues battle for the world championship.

READING ABOUT

Books

Goodman, Michael E. *The History of the Seattle Mariners.* Mankato, Minn.: The Creative Company, 2002.

Savage, Jeff. *Ichiro Suzuki.* Minneapolis, Minn.: Lerner Publishing Group, 2003.

Stewart, Mark. *Ichiro Suzuki: The Best in the West.* Brookfield, Conn.: Millbrook Press, 2002.

Internet Addresses

The Official Web Site of Major League Baseball
<http://mlb.com>

The Official Web Site of the Seattle Mariners
<http://seattle.mariners.mlb.com>

INDEX